Play, Play, Play, Dear Dragon

by Margaret Hillert
Illustrated by David Schimmell

NORWOOD HOUSE PRESS

DEAR CAREGIVER, The *Beginning-to-Read* series is a carefully written collection of classic readers you may remember from your own childhood. Each book features text comprised of common sight words to provide your child ample practice reading the words that appear most frequently in written text. The many additional details in the pictures enhance the story and offer the opportunity for you to help your child expand oral language and develop comprehension.

Begin by reading the story to your child, followed by letting him or her read familiar words and soon your child will be able to read the story independently. At each step of the way, be sure to praise your reader's efforts to build his or her confidence as an independent reader. Discuss the pictures and encourage your child to make connections between the story and his or her own life. At the end of the story, you will find reading activities and a word list that will help your child practice and strengthen beginning reading skills.

Above all, the most important part of the reading experience is to have fun and enjoy it!

Shannon Cannon

Shannon Cannon,
Literacy Consultant

Norwood House Press • P.O. Box 316598 • Chicago, Illinois 60631
For more information about Norwood House Press please visit our website at
www.norwoodhousepress.com or call 866-565-2900.

Text copyright ©2009 by Margaret Hillert. Illustrations and cover design copyright ©2009 by Norwood House Press, Inc. All rights reserved. No part of this book may be reproduced or utilized in any form or by any means without written permission from the publisher.
Designer: The Design Lab

LIBRARY OF CONGRESS CATALOGING-IN-PUBLICATION DATA

Hillert, Margaret.
 Play, play, play, dear dragon / Margaret Hillert ; illustrated by David Schimmell.
  p. cm. — (A beginning-to-read book)
 Summary: "A boy and his pet dragon spend a day at the playground and make a new friend"—Provided by publisher.
 ISBN-13: 978-1-59953-294-3 (library edition : alk. paper)
 ISBN-10: 1-59953-294-8 (library edition : alk. paper) [1.
Dragons—Fiction. 2. Playgrounds—Fiction.] I. Schimmell, David, ill. II. Title.
 PZ7.H558Pn 2009
 [E]—dc22   2008037512

Manufactured in the United States of America in North Mankato, Minnesota.
R149—112009

There is a spot where we can play.

I am up now.
You have to get up, too.
I want you with me.

Come on.
Come on.
One—two—three.
UPPPP—

5

I will eat this.
I like it.
It is good for me.

Have some of this.
It is good for you.
It will make you big.

Now we will find the spot
where we can play.

I see something.
I see it.
Run, run, run.

Go away.
You can not come up here.
I do not want you here.

I will go look for them.
I will find them.

I am sorry.
I want to be friends.
I want to play with you.

Yes, yes.
We can be friends.
We can go to a good spot
to play.

Oh, boy!
Do you see that?

We can go UP, UP, UP.

We can go DOWN,
        DOWN,
            DOWN.

This is fun, too.
It is fun to do this.

Now I will help you do this.

And you can help me.
I like to do this.

Can you do this?
Can you do it?
One, and two, and three—

Here is my ball.
I am good at this.
Do you want to play with me?
This is fun.

This is fun, too.

I have to go now.
My mother wants me.

Here you are with me.
And here I am with you.
What a good day, dear dragon.

The following activities support the findings of the National Reading Panel that determined the most effective components for reading instruction are: Phonemic Awareness, Phonics, Vocabulary, Fluency, and Text Comprehension.

Phonemic Awareness: The /ou/ sound

Sound Substitution: Say the words on the left to your child. Ask your child to repeat the word, changing the middle sound to the /**ou**/ sound.

moose = mouse	spat = spout	fund = found
grand = ground	catch = couch	shot = shout
pat = pout	load = loud	pond = pound
band = bound	horse= house	scoot = scout

Phonics: The letters o and u

1. Demonstrate how to form the letters **o** and **u** for your child.

2. Have your child practice writing **o** and **u** at least three times each.

3. Write down the following letters and spaces and ask your child to write the letters **o** and **u** on the spaces in each word:

gr_ _ nd	f_ _ nd	l_ _ d	c_ _ nt
s_ _ nd	_ _ t	m_ _ se	pr_ _ d
m_ _ th	fl_ _ r	r_ _ nd	h_ _ se

4. Ask your child to read each word.

Vocabulary: Making Words

1. Write the words "the playground" at the top of a piece of paper.

2. Write each letter in the words "the playground" on separate small pieces of paper.

3. Explain to your child that the letters in the words **the** and **playground** can be used to make new words.

4. Provide the following clues and help your child use the letters to make the correct words. Ask your child to write the words on the paper under "the playground".

- A word that describes what you can do for fun with your friends. (play)
- Where you plant seeds. (ground)
- What you do when you use money to buy something. (pay)
- A word used for weight. (pound)
- What you do when you get in bed. (lay)
- Something you use to carry things (like your food in the lunchroom). (tray)
- The color made by mixing white and black. (gray)
- Something you use to clean things. (rag)
- The part of your body that has hair, ears, and a face. (head)
- What you do when you look at the words and pictures in a book. (read)
- The shape of a circle. (round)

Fluency: Choral Reading

1. Reread the story with your child at least two more times while your child tracks the print by running a finger under the words as they are read. Ask your child to read the words he or she knows with you.

2. Reread the story aloud together. Be careful to read at a rate that your child can keep up with.

3. Repeat choral reading and allow your child to be the lead reader and ask him or her to change from a whisper to a loud voice while you follow along and change your voice.

Text Comprehension: Discussion Time

1. Ask your child to retell the sequence of events in the story.

2. To check comprehension, ask your child the following questions:
   - How do you think the boy felt on page 10 when the other boy told him he couldn't come up?
   - How did the problem get solved?
   - What is your favorite thing to do at the playground?
   - How do you make new friends?
   - What was your favorite part of the story? Why?

***Play, Play, Play, Dear Dragon* uses the 70 words listed below.**
This list can be used to practice reading the words that appear in the text. You
may wish to write the words on index cards and use them to help your child
build automatic word recognition. Regular practice with these words will
enhance your child's fluency in reading connected text.

a	dragon	it	play	up
am				
and	eat	like	run	want(s)
are		look		was
at	find		see	we
away	for	make	some	what
	friends	me	something	where
ball	fun	mother	sorry	will
be		my	spot	with
big	get			
boy	go	no	that	yes
	good	not	the	you
can		now	them	
come	have		there	
	help	of	this	
dear	here	oh	three	
day		on	to	
do	I	one	too	
down	is		two	

ABOUT THE AUTHOR Margaret Hillert has written over 80 books for
children who are just learning to read. Her books
have been translated into many different languages and over a million children
throughout the world have read her books. She first started writing poetry as
a child and has continued to write for children and adults throughout her life. A
first grade teacher for 34 years, Margaret is now retired from teaching and lives in
Michigan where she likes to write, take walks in the morning, and care for her three cats.

Photograph by Glenna Washburn

ABOUT THE ADVISER Shannon Cannon contributed the activities pages that appear in
this book. Shannon serves as a literacy consultant and provides
staff development to help improve reading instruction. She is a frequent presenter at educational
conferences and workshops. Prior to this she worked as an elementary school teacher and as
president of a curriculum publishing company.